CONTENTS

MEET GEORGE AND HAROLD

Meet George Beard and Harold Hutchins. George is the kid on the left with the tie and the flat-top. Harold is the one on the right with the T-shirt and the bad haircut. Remember that now.

George and Harold were best friends. They had a lot in common. They lived right next door to each other and they were both in the same fourth-grade class at Jerome Horwitz Elementary School.

George and Harold were usually responsible kids. Whenever anything bad happened, George and Harold were usually responsible.

But don't get the wrong idea about these two. George and Harold were actually very nice boys. No matter what everybody else thought, they were good, sweet, and lovable. . . Well, OK, maybe they weren't so sweet and lovable, but they were good nonetheless.

It's just that George and Harold each had a "silly streak" a *kilometre* long. Usually that silly streak was hard to control. Sometimes it got them into trouble. But most of the time it was just a lot of fun. So turn the page for tons of silliness, a bit of trouble and loads of underpants!

"Knock knock?"
"Who's there?"
"I'm a pile-up."
"I'm a pile-up who?"
"No, you're not! Don't be so hard on yourself, buddy!"

Q) What did the mummy buffalo say to the baby buffalo when he went off to school?

A) Bison.

Q) What does lightning wear beneath its clothes?

A) Thunderwear.

Q) What should you do if you get swallowed by an elephant?

A) Jump up and down until you're all pooped out.

Q) Why did Batman cross his legs?

A) He had to go to the bat-room.

Q) If you had fifty bananas in one hand, and twenty-five litres of ice-cream in the other, what would you have?

A) Really big hands.

Guess What Time it is?!?
PRANK TIME
It's Time To Learn A Fun Prank!
-With George And Harold

All you Need is A Funnel, A penny, A glass of Water...
...And A Victim!!!
BLAH
BLAH
BLAH

First, Stick The Little end of The Funnel into your Pants.

NOW, PRETEND YOU'RE PLAYING A FUN GAME!
HA-HA-HA
CLINK
HEY! WHAT'S GOING ON OVER THERE?!!?

IT'S A FUN GAME. YOU TRY TO DROP A PENNY OFF OF YOUR CHIN AND CATCH IT IN THE FUNNEL. IT'S REALLY HARD!

OH YEAH?!!? WELL LET ME TRY IT, BUB!
OK!

When your victim leans back to put the penny on his chin...

HOW TO DRAW MR KRUPP

1.

2.

3.

4.

5.

6.

7.

8.

9.

10.

11.

12.

13.

14.

15.

16.

DOG MAN in The TONGUE OF JUSTICE

DOG Man was The Greatest Cop ever!!!

BUT he had some Bad Habits.
cheeF

He Dranked out of the TOYLET.

He Licked him-self in inapro-preate plases.

and he threw up everywhere.
cheeF

BLAP
cheeF

to be continued. . .

Q) Why do sharks live in salt water?

A) Because pepper water makes them sneeze.

Q) How do you make a tissue dance?

A) Put a little boogie into it.

Q) Why did Tigger stick his head in the toilet?

A) He was looking for "Pooh".

Q) Who is Peter Pan's worst-smelling friend?

A) Stinkerbell.

Q) What nationality are you when you go to the bathroom?

A) European.

A woman walks into a pet store and says, "Can I get a puppy for my daughter?" "Sorry, lady," says the pet store owner. "We don't do swaps."

Wedgie Woman's Bad Hair Day

Tame the Mane!

George And Harold's College O' ART

MAKE YOUR OWN FLIP-O-RAMA!!!

First You need An ordinary A4 Piece of paper.

Got it!

Now fold the top half of your paper over the picture you've just drawn.

NOW we're going to do some tracing on the top page. The 1st Rule is: If you DON'T want something to move, **TRACE IT!!!**

You don't want the floor to move, do you?
Nope! So I'll TRACE it.

Do you want his legs or torso to move?
Nope! So I'll TRACE 'em.

What about his head?
Nope! So I'll TRACE it.

How 'bout his ARms?
Hmmm... his Right ARm shoudn't move, so I'll TRACe it.

But his Left ARm is dRibbling the bALL, so it should probAbly move A Little, huh?
Yep!

So I'LL Re-dRAW his Left ARm in A NEW POSITION!

HAROLD has just shown the **2nd** Rule of FLIP-O-RAMA: If you WANT something to move, you must **RE-DRAW** it in a new position.

★ Look at HAROLD'S two drawings below... Notice the differences.

FIRST DRAWING (BOTTOM PAGE)	SECOND DRAWING (TOP PAGE)

Now flip the top page up and down to try it out.
Hey! It WORKS!!!
FLIP
FLIP
FLIP

NoTe: When flipping your home-made FLIP-O-RAMAS, ONLY flip The Top Page. ALSO, MAKE SURE That you can see both pictures AS you FLIP.
Top page flips up and down.
BOTTOM PAGE STAYS FLAT.
Hold here.

You might need some Adjustments To make it work better.

I'm going to draw Action Lines on The Top page.

Hey Kids---Try making your own Flip-O-Rama!!!

SPEShel NOTES FOR FLiP-O-RAMISTS

1. Typing paper and notebook paper work best.

2. Although you need to trace, don't use tracing paper. It will ruin the Affect.

3. Grown-ups will freak out if your flip-O-Ramas Feacher "people" beating each other up. To get around this, draw robots and monsters instead. (For some REASon, Grown-ups think thats O.K. ...Go Figure!)

4. You can get good ideas by studying the Flip-O-RamAS in The "CAptain UNderpants" and "Ricky Ricotta" Books.

HERE COMES THE BAT, MAN!

Now try creating your own Flip-O-Rama. Draw a villain here.
Make him about the same height as Captain Underpants.

HERE COMES THE BAT, MAN!

Draw your villain here. Follow the instructions in George and Harold's College O' Art to decide which parts of your drawing to change.

FINAL EXAM

Hi everybody! One thing I know for sure is that kids LOVE to study and take tests! That's why we've included this incredibly difficult FINAL EXAM! Make sure you've studied George and Harold's College O' Art comic before you begin. Good luck!

1. What's the best paper for Flip-O-Rama?

a) note paper

b) toilet paper

c) some scraps of cardboard from a cereal box

2. If you can't see your drawing through the paper, you should ____.

a) ask a friend to describe it for you

b) put a box over your head

c) hold it up to the window

3. When flipping your homemade Flip-o-ramas, you should only flip ____.

a) the top page

b) a pancake

c) a coin

4. Don't worry about making mistakes. That's why they invented ____.

a) lawyers

b) erasers

c) soap-on-a-rope

5. If you have trouble writing action scenes, you can always use ___.

a) a ghost writer

b) Flip-O-Rama

c) egg salad

6. You can get ideas for your Flip-O-Ramas by studying ____.

a) your maths homework

b) recipe books

c) Captain Underpants books

7. What's the world's EASIEST Flip-O-Rama?

a) a guy with a chicken up his nose

b) a guy with a basketball

c) a guy with a basketball up his nose

8. The FIRST rule of Flip-O-Rama is: If you don't want something to move, _____.

a) trace it

b) put it in a "time-out"

c) threaten to stop the car

9. The SECOND rule of Flip-O-Rama is: If you want something to move, you must _____.

a) make rude noises with your armpits

b) drink lots of prune juice

c) re-draw it in a new position

10. The more you practise, _____.

a) the better you get

b) the dumber you get

c) the stinkier you get

Turn the page for answers!

ANSWERS:
1: a, 2: c, 3: a, 4: b, 5: b,
6: c, 7: b, 8: a, 9: c, 10: a

If you got at least 6 right, CONGRATULATIONS! You've just graduated from George and Harold's College o' Art.

CAN YOU ESCAPE DOCTOR NAPPY'S DEVASTATING NAPPY OF DOOM?

The Tongue of Justice Part 2

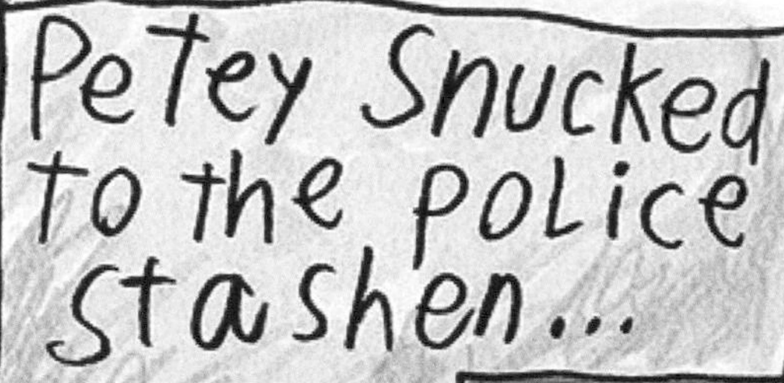

Hello?

theres a Bank robbery

The cops ran to their cars.
wee-ooo-wee-ooo-we
ZOOM!
But then...
cheef
Sniff
Sniff
cheef
must OBEY Petey
Soon every cop Becamed a mindless zombie...

to be continued...

Hello kiddies! I've taken my terrifying Name Change-O-Chart 2000 and turned it into a WORD search PUZZLE! Try to find all the names from the chart below in the puzzle on the right. Look up, down, across and backwards!

FIRST CHART: USE the FIRST LETTER of YOUR FIRST NAME To DETERMINE YOUR **NEW** FIRST NAME!

A= STINKY
B= LUMPY
C= Buttercup
D= Gidget
E= CRUSTY
F= GREASY
G= FLUFFY
H= Cheeseball
I= Chim-Chim
J= Poopsie
K= Flunky
L= Booger
M= Pinky
N= Zippy
O= GOOBER
P= DooFus
Q= SLIMY
R= LOOPY
S= Snotty
T= FALAFEL
U= DORKY
V= Squeezit
W= OPRAH
X= Skipper
Y= Dinky
Z= ZSA-ZSA

L	U	M	P	Y	U	M	T	E	Y
L	O	O	P	Y	S	I	C	I	K
A	S	Z	A	S	Z	H	R	S	N
B	U	T	T	E	R	C	U	P	I
E	H	S	L	R	J	M	S	O	D
S	Q	U	E	E	Z	I	T	O	G
E	Y	F	F	P	I	H	Y	P	R
E	F	O	A	P	P	C	F	R	E
H	F	O	L	I	P	L	L	A	A
C	U	D	A	K	Y	G	U	H	S
I	L	G	F	S	T	I	N	K	Y
F	F	Y	K	R	O	D	K	V	M
S	N	P	B	L	M	G	Y	D	I
R	E	B	O	O	G	E	R	L	L
P	I	N	K	Y	T	T	O	N	S

HOW TO DRAW CAPTAIN UNDERPANTS

1.

2.

3.

4.

5.

6.

7.

8.

9.

10.

11.

12.

13.

14.

15.

16.

THE CAFETERIA LADIES' CRAZY CROSSWORD

Fill in the answers in the grid, one letter in each square.

Across

3. Dr _____ was defeated soon after George shot fake doggy doo-doo at him.
5. *The Attack of the _____ Toilets*.
6. Watch out for the Equally Evil Lunchroom _____ Nerds.
8. Pippy P. Poopypants invented the _____ Jogger 2000.
10. "Hooray for Captain _____!"
11. Don't drink the Evil Zombie Nerd _____!
13. Captain Underpants often shouts "_____-La-Laaaaa!"
14. *Cheesy Animation Technology* is more commonly known as _____-O-Rama.

Down

1. *The Adventures of _____ Underpants*.
2. Mr Krupp was transformed into a superhero by the 3-D Hypno-______.
4. *The Perilous Plot of ____ Poopypants*.
7. Zorx, Klax and Jennifer were evil guys from outer ______.
9. A popular way to misspell the word "laughs".
12. Captain Underpants wears a red _____.

Calling all Zombie Cops!

meet me at Petey's secrit Lab...

...and make it snappy!!!
Yes, master Petey! we will OBEY!!!
cheef

Dog Man chased Petey all Across town...

...and into his secrit Lab.
peteys secrit LAB

Up the stairs
they ran.

Dog man was getting Super thirsty...

Then he saw it!!!

gLissening...
sparkeLing...
Refreshing...

COOL as a mounten Streem...

Thirst Qwench-ing and DeLish-ess...

GLUG GLUG
GLUG

Aaaaaaah!

DOG man ran up to the next Floor......

where a BIG Suprise AWAITED for him.

HAW HAW HAW!!!
cheef

to be continued...

WELCOME TO A BRAND-NEW CAPTAIN UNDERPANTS STORY. . . AND YOU'RE THE STAR!

Before you read the story on the following pages, fill in all the blanks with appropriate words. Below each blank is a small description of the type of word you need to write.

For example, if the blank looks like this:

______________, you would think up an adjective and put it
(an adjective)

in the blank like this: ______stinky______ .
(an adjective)

Remember, DON'T read the story first. It's more fun if you go through and fill in the blanks first, THEN read the story.

When you're done, follow the instructions at the bottom of each page to complete the illustrations.

JUST FOR REMINDERS:
a **Verb** is an action word (like jump, swim, kick, squish, run, etc.)
an **Adjective** is a word that describes a person, place or thing (lumpy, dumb, purple, hairy, etc.)

CAPTAIN UNDERPANTS VS THE EVIL MONSTER

(STARRING GEORGE, HAROLD AND YOU!)

Once upon a time, George, Harold and their friend,

__________________, were busy studying about the
(your name)

wonders of __________________ __________________,
(an adjective) (disgusting things)

when their new science teacher, Mr __________________,
(a funny name)

accidentally spilled some __________________
(a gross adjective)

__________________ on a pile of toxic __________________.
(a liquid) (silly things)

(Draw yourself sitting here)

(Draw the teacher spilling liquid on to some toxic stuff)

Suddenly, the pile began to morph into

a giant, evil ___________________ .
(a silly thing)

"Help," cried _____________________, "a
(somebody in your class)

giant, evil ______________________________
(the silly thing you just used above)

just stepped on my lunchbox and ate up

_____________________!"
(your gym teacher's name)

"Oh NO!" cried Mr Krupp. "The poor

lunchbox!"

(Draw the giant, evil monster)

(Draw the kid in your class)

George, Harold and ______________________ tried to
(your name)

escape by hiding behind a ______________________ .
(a very small thing)

Then ______________________ snapped ______________________
(your name) (either "his" or "her")

fingers.

Soon, a ______________________ grin came across
(an adjective)

Mr Krupp's face as he dropped his ______________________
(an adjective)

______________________ and ran to his office.
(an article of clothing)

(Draw yourself)

(Draw the thing you're all hiding behind)

(Draw the giant, evil monster)

Soon, Captain Underpants ____________________ (an action verb ending in "ed") through the wall. He grabbed a ____________________ (an adjective) ________________ (a thing) and hit the monster on its ________________ (a body part).

"Ouchies!" screamed the monster. It turned and ____________________ (a fight move ending in "ed") Captain Underpants on his ________________ (a body part).

(Draw yourself)

(Draw the monster fighting Captain Underpants)

_____________________ quickly mixed up a bottle of
(your name)

____________________________ with a jar of toxic,
(something a kid would drink)

_______________________ _______________________ .
(an adjective) (disgusting things)

"Hey, _______________________ ," said George, "where'd
(your name)

you find that jar of crazy stuff?!!?"

"It was right here next to this barrel of toxic

_______________________ _______________________ ," said
(an adjective) (different disgusting things)

_______________________ .
(your name)

"Oh," said Harold. "That makes sense."

____

(Draw yourself creating a strange mixture)

(Draw the contents of the barrel coming out the top)

_______________ shook up the strange mixture and
(your name)

threw it at the monster.

"_______________!" screamed the monster as
(something you might scream or cheer)

it fell over and died of a massive _______________ attack.
(a body part)

"That makes sense, too," said George.

Unfortunately, some of the mixture splashed on Captain Underpants's head, and he turned back into Mr Krupp.

(Draw yourself throwing the strange concoction on to the monster)

(Draw the monster getting splashed)

"HOLY ______________ (an adjective) ______________ (silly animals)!"

shouted Mr Krupp. "I'll bet that George, Harold and

______________ (your name) are responsible for this mess!" So he

punished the three kids by making them ______________ (an action verb)

in the ______________ (a room in the school) for ______________ (a number) hours.

"This has got to be the dumbest story we've ever been in," said George.

"Don't blame me," said Harold. "______________ (your name) wrote it!"

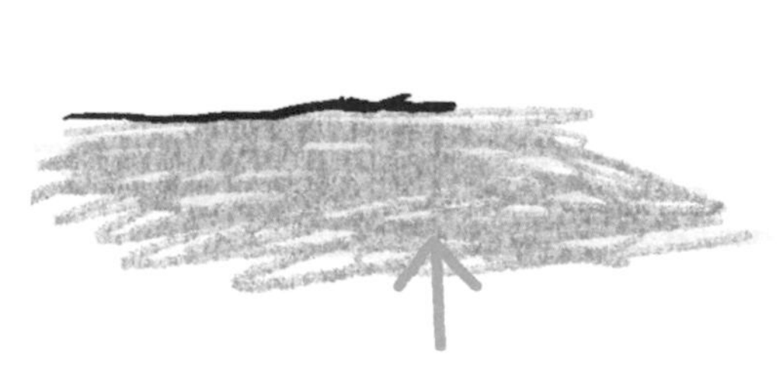

(Draw yourself looking guilty)

The Tongue of Justice Part 4

Dog Man had to act fast! So He thought up a 3-Step plan.

Triple Flip-O-Ramas

animate the action cheesily. Heres How:

Hold Book Open Like this...

Flip Page Back and Forth.

add your own sound afecks!

Left Hand Here

step 2

collect the antidote

step 3

apply the antidote

RighT Thum Here

Step 1

Retreeve the antidote

Step 2

Collect the antidote

DOG Man Licked all cops Faces.

and soon...
Hey!
cheef

we aint zom-Bies no more!!!
aw, man!

Aint you Glad you ain't no zombie no more?
I shure amn't!

HORAY FOR DOG Man!!!
cheef
Rats!

THE END

YUM YUM EAT 'EM UP
A TALKING TOILET MAZE

ANSWERS

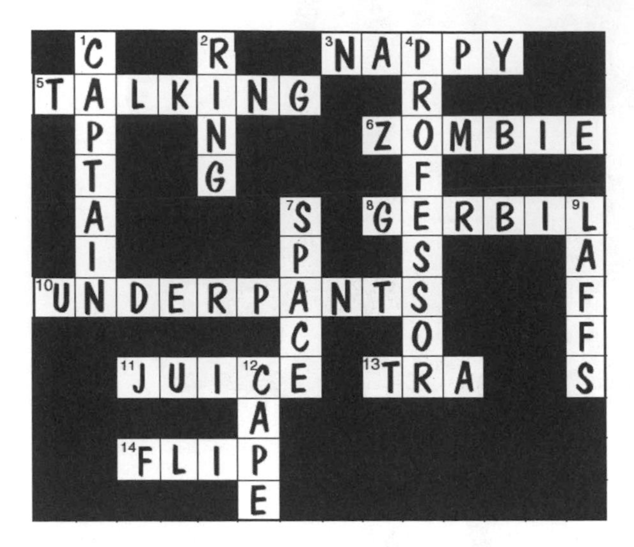

CROSSWORD P. 43

L	U	M	P	Y	U	M	T	E	Y
L	O	O	P	Y	S	I	C	I	K
A	S	Z	A	S	Z	H	R	S	N
B	U	T	T	E	R	C	U	P	I
E	H	S	L	R	J	M	S	O	D
S	Q	U	E	E	Z	I	T	O	G
E	Y	F	F	P	I	H	Y	P	R
E	F	O	A	P	P	C	F	R	E
H	F	O	L	I	P	L	L	A	A
C	U	D	A	K	Y	G	U	H	S
I	L	G	F	S	T	I	N	K	Y
F	F	Y	K	R	O	D	K	V	M
S	N	P	B	L	M	G	Y	D	I
R	E	B	O	O	G	E	R	L	L
P	I	N	K	Y	T	T	O	N	S

WORD SEARCH P. 39

MAZE P. 61

MAZE P. 33

MAZE P. 16